VANISH

LYNN SHANNON

VANISH

Copyright © 2018 by Lynn Balabanos

Published by Creative Thoughts, LLC

All rights reserved.

No part of this book may be reproduced in any form or by any electronic or mechanical means, including information storage and retrieval systems, without written permission from the author, except for the use of brief quotations in a book review.

This book is a work of fiction. Names, characters, businesses, organizations, places, events and incidents either are the product of the author's imagination or are used factitiously. Any resemblance to actual persons, living or dead, events, or locales is entirely coincidental.

Scripture appearing in this novel in whole or in part from THE HOLY BIBLE, NEW INTERNATIONAL VERSION®, NIV® Copyright © 1973, 1978, 1984, 2011 by Biblica, Inc.™ Used by permission. All rights reserved worldwide.

This book is dedicated to Eva. We both worked for years toward our different dreams, supporting each other every step of the way. We made it, my friend. I'm glad we could do it together.

"For I know the plans I have for you," declares the Lord, "plans to prosper you and not harm you, plans to give you hope and a future."

JEREMIAH 29:11

ONE

Home renovations were going to get her killed.

Janet West white-knuckled the steering wheel. Rain pounded against the windshield and obscured her vision of the country road. In the space between the seats, a heap of different bathroom tiles mingled with the strap of her purse and a collection of paint color samples.

A whimper rose from the passenger seat. Callie, her golden retriever mix, cast a worried glance at her.

"I know, I know," Janet said. "I spent too long in the hardware store before picking you up at the vet. I got carried away."

Her headlights were no match for the storm and she flipped on her brights. Lightning flashed, followed by a window-rattling boom of thunder. Callie whimpered again and pushed her body against the seat. The poor dog was shaking.

"Five minutes and we'll be home, girl."

The farmhouse didn't feel like home yet with its peeling plaster and horrific bathrooms, but after this week of renovations, Janet hoped it would.

"Todd should still be there, finishing up the kitchen backsplash. I'm sure you can convince him to sneak you a cookie."

Callie's tail thumped at Todd's name. Her dog had fallen in love with him from the moment he'd set foot on the property. Not that Janet could blame her. Todd Duncan was ruggedly handsome and possessed both a quiet strength and an innate kindness she couldn't resist either.

"What am I going to do with you when he leaves, huh?" she asked. "You know he's only hanging around to finish construction on the house. Afterward, he's moving on to his next adventure."

The conversation was as much for Janet as it was for Callie. It wouldn't do either of them any good to get attached to a man with one foot out the door.

Another bolt of lightning lit up the sky. Swollen ditches on either side struggled to keep up with the torrential downpour. Janet leaned closer to the windshield. She hadn't missed the turn off for her drive, had she?

Something dashed into the road from the opposite side and she stomped on the brakes. The headlights reflected off fabric and a pale face.

Janet swerved.

Her head bounced against the side panel. The

backend of her SUV fishtailed, skimming across the flooded asphalt, and a thump resounded against the side of the vehicle. She turned into the spin and pumped the brakes. Her heart pounded, the sound of it roaring in her ears, while the blur of trees beyond her windshield rushed closer. Janet's body tensed, preparing to crash.

The tires found traction. The SUV slid to a stop inches from the deep ditch lining the side of the road. Rain battered against the roof. Something slick and warm trickled down her head.

She sat, stunned and motionless.

A wet nose nudged her arm. Janet sucked in a deep breath. She pried her fingers from the steering wheel and shoved the vehicle into park. Callie strained against the harness securing her to the seat and nudged Janet's arm again.

"Are you okay, girl?"

She patted the dog with one hand and used the other to check her scalp. She winced as pain shot across her head. The wet liquid coating her fingers was inky-black in the weak light coming off her headlights.

Blood. On her hands.

With a jolt, Janet's gaze shot to the rearview mirror. A barely discernible lump lay on the road.

No, no, no, no, no.

She flung her door open. Raindrops pelted her bare head and ran down her face in rivets, instantly soaking her. Goosebumps broke out across her skin. As if on autopilot, Janet flipped the hood of her coat up. She grabbed the flashlight from the side pocket with a shaking hand and raced toward the lump. Water soaked her tennis shoes, numbing her toes, and her breath came in short spurts.

Her flashlight flickered over a pale hand lying stark against the blacktop. Janet's heart thundered and chills raced down her spine. *Oh, God, no.* It hadn't been a nightmare.

The closer she ran, the more her light revealed. Ankle boots covered in mud and grass, soaked slacks, and a pale silk blouse. The woman's wrists were rubbed raw, the skin broken and bloody, and a large purple bruise bloomed on her cheek.

Janet's knees hit the pavement with bone-jarring force. Her whole body trembled. She placed her fingers along the smooth column of the woman's throat.

She couldn't find a pulse. A sob rose in her throat. She yanked the cell phone from her pocket and dialed 911.

Her phone beeped. And then nothing.

She had no signal. Tears ran down her face, mixing with the rain. She hit the buttons again. "Come on, come on!"

Fingers grasped her arm. Janet gasped and tumbled back. The flashlight fell from her hand and rolled a short distance before coming to a stop.

The woman on the road groaned.

Panic gave way to heady relief and Janet ripped off her jacket, spreading it across the woman's torso. It was poor protection from the rain, but it was something. The woman grabbed her arm again, her chipped and jagged fingernails digging into Janet's skin. Her dark eyes were wide. Desperate. Her mouth moved, but no sound came out.

"You're hurt." Janet's voice came out steady and sure, a far cry from the tangled emotions inside her. "I'm going to get help."

She glanced back at her SUV. Her cell phone didn't work, but she had an in-vehicle safety and security system. It was able to contact emergency services, even in most dead zones.

The woman tugged on her arm again, yanking Janet toward her. Up close, the lines on her face were visible. Her hair was gray at the roots, as if she normally dyed it but hadn't in several months. Again her mouth moved. Janet couldn't make out what she was saying.

"You're going to be okay." She worked her hand free. "I'm going to call for help, but I'll be right back."

In the distance, a dog barked. Lightning lit up the sky, as bright as day. The woman's gaze flickered to something behind Janet. Her eyes widened.

Janet was yanked backward, lifted off the ground against a wall of hard muscle. A scream rose in her throat, muffled before it could pass her lips by a cloth closing over her nose and mouth. A pungent, musty odor filled her nostrils. The arm across her waist trapped her hands next to her body. She flailed her feet, landing a solid kick with her tennis shoe into a shin. Her attacker grunted. The dog barking grew furious.

The vise around her waist tightened, the man's hold

unrelenting. She couldn't breathe. Her vision darkened. Janet bit the fabric covering her mouth, but only got cloth and not the flesh of her attacker's hand.

Everything went black.

TWO

Todd wiped a bit of grout off the backsplash, his attention drifting toward the window in the back door and the empty carport nearby. The deluge had relented to a steady drizzle. A tree branch had fallen on the far side of the yard, narrowly missing the storage sheds. It lay discarded in the grass, the jagged edge dangerously sharp, pine needles quivering in the wind. A silent testament to the dangers of being out in a thunderstorm. Todd's hand tightened on the cloth.

Where was Janet?

She'd left the hardware store before the storm, but even if she pulled over to wait it out, she should've been back by now. He unhooked his cell phone from his belt and dialed her number. No answer.

His pulse elevated and his stomach grew queasy. This was the third time he'd tried to call and she hadn't answered. The image of his parents' destroyed sedan, the body dented and damaged, being pulled out of a ditch flashed in his mind. They hadn't made it out alive.

Todd closed his eyes and took a deep breath. He needed to be reasonable. The county was full of dead zones. Janet could be driving through one, or she'd made another stop somewhere and lost track of time. There could be any number of reasons why she was late. Even as he talked himself through it, he was moving toward his truck in the driveway.

The springs protested when his weight landed in the front seat and the engine wheezed and rattled like it was on its last breath. Probably was. Todd could afford to replace it many times over, but sentimentality held him back. The old beast had carried him through thousands of miles while he crisscrossed the country, seeing every nook and cranny. The restless feeling plaguing him after his parents' death only let up when he was on the move. The army had been good for travel, and after the service, he'd never spent longer than six months in any one place.

That was until Sweetgrass.

He'd been here eight months, most of it spent working on the West family ranch. He should've left months ago, but seeing the condition of the old farmhouse, he'd known Janet would need experienced help. Todd justified it because it meant earning extra cash, but his bank account didn't need the padding. No, he'd been unable to leave for a far simpler reason. He hadn't wanted to let go of their friendship yet.

At the end of the drive, he hesitated. There were two roads leading from Janet's property into town. One was more commonly used, better paved and connected with the freeway. The other was worn and tired, more of a farm road, but it was a shortcut from the hardware store.

He headed for the farm road. If she'd had an accident, it would take forever for someone to notice her there. His windshield wipers swiped away the drizzle. Clouds hung low and dangerous, promising the reprieve from the rain was brief. He took a wide curve and hit the brakes.

Janet's SUV sat on the road, the back-end inches from a flooded ditch. The driver's side door hung open. A dog was howling. Callie. The sound was mournful, low, and sent shivers down Todd's spine. He shoved his truck into park and got out. Rain tapped against the brim of his ball cap and drizzled down into his shirt.

Callie caught sight of him. She stopped howling and gave three short yips. Todd's boots slid to a stop. Janet's rain jacket lay in the middle of the road, a puddle of red against the dark asphalt. It looked like blood. His legs went weak, his feet faltering.

Lord, no. Please, not Janet.

He sucked in a sharp breath and held it as he moved around the side of the SUV's door. Janet was hunched over the steering wheel. Her curly hair was tangled. Trails of blood crept along one cheekbone, the color exaggerated by her pallid skin. Her eyes were open, but she appeared to be staring at nothing.

A sharp stab of pain jabbed him in the chest, close enough to his heart to feel like it was breaking. He grabbed the SUV door as his military training kicked in. He scanned her and realized her chest was moving.

She was breathing. *Thank you, Lord.*

Had she been in a car accident? The SUV appeared undamaged. Was it just the bump on her head?

"Janet?" He placed a hand on her upper arm. Her sweater was sopping wet. "Are you okay?"

She jerked in her seat. A fist swung toward his face. Todd reacted instinctively by dodging it. She screamed and launched from the vehicle like a wild woman. He backed up, trying to deflect her attack while not hurting her.

"Janet, stop!"

She pushed him toward the other side of the road. Her eyes were open, but it was like she wasn't seeing him. A knot tightened in his stomach. She landed two solid punches on his upraised arms, hard enough to bruise flesh. He didn't care about his own, but she would damage her knuckles.

He caught her wrists, grasping them gently. "Janet! It's me—Todd."

She froze. Blinked. Blinked again. She inhaled a sharp breath as recognition flitted across her pretty features.

"Todd." His name came out on a whisper. Her body sagged, and if he hadn't been holding her, she would've sunk to the ground. "I—"

The word cut off on a sob. He pulled her against his chest and her soaked clothes wet his own. What had happened? Janet's raincoat lay nearby on the road, and a sick thought occurred to him. His body heat rose, but Todd tamped down the anger when she trembled in his arms. He needed to stay calm.

"It's okay. I've got you." He wrapped the ends of his jacket around her, a shield against the rain and cold. "You're safe now."

She stiffened and pushed away violently, knocking him off balance. "Where is she?"

He frowned. "Where's who?"

She raced forward a few steps. Todd followed, but she bounced around the road like a ping pong ball in an arcade machine. Callie, still strapped in the vehicle, sensed her master's emotional turmoil and started howling.

"Where is she?"

Janet stumbled and lifted a shaking hand to her head before bending at the waist and heaving. He closed the distance between them, lifting her hair out of the way. Todd had no idea what was happening, but his first priority was to take care of her.

"You need to go to the hospital."

"No." Janet sucked in a breath and pointed to her discarded raincoat. "She was right there. He took her."

She wasn't making any sense. How hard had she hit her head? Concussions weren't anything to play around with and all the symptoms pointed to one.

Her gaze lifted. Met his. Hidden in their depths, amid the seaside-blue, there was terror. An icy cold finger touched the back of his neck.

"We need to call the police, Todd. Right now."

THREE

Beams of early morning sunlight streamed through the kitchen windows, making patterns along the tile floor and the new backsplash. Janet swallowed two painkillers and chased them with a sip of coffee. The warm liquid traced a path to her belly but failed to ease the coldness in her bones or the lingering sense of vulnerability and worry.

Yesterday had been a whirlwind of doctors and tests and questions by the police. They hadn't found the woman. They didn't even know her name, but the haunting image of her face appeared all night in Janet's dreams. She sent up a prayer for the woman's safety. Another one. What hours she hadn't spent sleeping, she'd been talking with God.

She glanced in the backyard but didn't see Callie. Carrying her coffee mug, she went to the windows overlooking the front of the house. A familiar beat-up truck with a dented driver's side door and rusted chrome sat in her unpaved driveway. Her dog circled, sniffing the tires.

What in the world?

Crisp air stole her breath and her wading boots thudded against the wooden planks of the old porch. The front seat in the truck was tilted back. Todd's eyes were closed, his leather jacket caressing his broad shoulders. Bristles covered his strong jaw and he was wearing the same flannel shirt from yesterday. She rapped on the window and he jolted upright, whacking his head against the handle over the door. Janet winced.

"Sorry," she said as he opened the door. "I didn't mean to startle you. What are you doing here?"

"Standing guard." He rubbed his head and yawned. "You don't have a security system yet, and with everything that happened yesterday, I figured it wouldn't hurt to have extra eyes on the house."

Heat radiated through her chest. He'd stayed with her through everything yesterday and now this... "Todd, you didn't have to."

"I know." He took the mug from her hand and drained it before flashing her a smile. The dimple in his left cheek winked. "You make the best coffee. Don't suppose there's more where this came from, is there?"

Her lips twitched. "I've got a whole pot with your name on it."

They were on the porch when Callie let out a bark and streaked off. A Sweetgrass Police Department SUV turned into her drive. Janet whistled, calling her dog back, as Chief Rod Jackman climbed out. Mid-forties with a shaved head and a fondness for aviator sunglasses, he'd taken over as police chief last year. His reputation was solid, but his choice in employees made her leery.

Her spine stiffened when the passenger side of the SUV opened and the reason for her misgivings came into view. Winston Maxwell had a wad of Skoal tucked in the bottom of his lip and spat out a stream of dark spittle before swaggering around the vehicle. His handsome good looks were offset by a rattlesnake's temperament. She'd done her best to avoid him, but it seemed her luck had run out.

Shaking off the bad vibe, she focused on Chief Jackman. "Any news?"

"Not yet, but I have a few follow-up questions to ask, if you don't mind." He nodded to Todd standing nearby. "Duncan."

"What questions?" Janet asked.

"Ain't you gonna invite us inside?" Winston rested his hand on the butt of his gun. He glanced at the mug in Todd's hand. "I hope Southern hospitality hasn't disappeared."

The idea of him anywhere inside her house made her skin crawl.

"My house is a mess at the moment because of the construction." She tilted her chin up. "Here's fine."

Todd slanted a glance in her direction, his brow furrowed. It wasn't like her to be rude and he knew it. He edged closer until the two of them were side by side.

"Suit yourself." Chief Jackman removed a piece of paper from a manila folder in his hand. "Are you sure this is the woman you saw on the road yesterday?"

He flipped it around. Janet's breath caught. The sketch artist she'd worked with from the sheriff's department had managed to capture the woman's features, as well as her sense of terror.

"It's her." She tore her gaze away from the rendering to study the chief's expression. His eyes were hidden behind the sunglasses, but his mouth was in a tight line. "Why?"

"She's not a local and no one matching her description has been reported missing in the county for the last twenty years."

"What does that mean?" Todd asked.

"It means we don't have an ID on her. I've had search dogs out to the location where the incident took place. They didn't pick up on anything. Normally I'd assume it was because the perpetrator transported her by car, but you didn't see or hear a vehicle." He gestured toward the road. "Your property is on one side and on the other is Mabel Bertrand. She didn't see or hear anything."

"Mrs. Bertrand is ninety years old. I'd be surprised if she *had* heard or seen anything." Janet crossed her arms over her chest. "It doesn't mean someone didn't cut across her property."

"Then the dogs would have picked up on it." Winston's mouth twitched, and he rocked on his heels. "If you need to tell us something, now would be the time?"

Heat flooded Janet's veins and rose in her cheeks. Beside her, Todd stiffened. "Are you accusing her of lying?"

"Hold on, hold on." The chief lifted his sunglasses and shot his officer a dirty look before focusing back on Janet. "Let's not go off the deep end here. Listen, the tox screen at the hospital didn't show anything in your system. However, you did hit your head when your vehicle fishtailed. That kind of injury can cause a person to hallucinate—"

She smacked her hand against the porch railing. "I did not hallucinate her. I did not dream up the attack or being drugged."

She closed her eyes. She was letting her temper get the best of her. Not a great way to convince them she was telling the truth.

But it was just so *insulting*.

The woman's face flashed in her mind. Janet sucked in a breath and let it out slowly. "Listen, I know the story sounds crazy and there are things I can't explain, but Chief, the woman is real. She had rope burns on her wrists and bruises on her face. I think she's in serious danger."

"Unfortunately, at the moment, I have no physical evidence collaborating your version of events." He placed his sunglasses back on his face. "Until I do, there's nothing else for me to investigate."

The two men ambled to their vehicle, and she watched them go with a burning knot in her belly.

They might not investigate, but she would.

This was far from over.

FOUR

Todd pried his fingers from around the coffee mug and flexed them. He was surprised it hadn't shattered in his hand, grinding into pieces of dust under the force of his anger. Those jokers were the town's law enforcement? He wouldn't put them in charge of a neighborhood watch group, let alone a police department.

He slid a glance at Janet out of the corner of his eye. Her curly hair was loose, framing her face and highlighting the color in her cheeks. Shadows from a restless night's sleep marred the skin under her eyes and her lips were flattened into a hard line. She turned to go back inside the house.

"I know that look," Todd said, following. "It's the same one you get when we fight about the construction and you're determined to get your way."

Inside, it smelled like a mixture of cinnamon, sugar, and fresh coffee. Tarps were spread over the furniture in the living room, and several paint color samples graced one wall. Callie bolted in. Janet grabbed her before she could cross the house.

Taking a towel from the coat hook, she wiped the dog's feet. "I refuse to accept nothing can be done to identify the woman or find her."

He shrugged out of his jacket. "What about your brother? Isn't he in law enforcement?"

"Yes, but Grady's recovering from a gunshot wound in Nashville with my older sister. I don't want to involve him if I can avoid it. I could go to the sheriff's department, but I'm not sure they would take my side over the police chief's anyway. Law enforcement tends to stick together."

She rose from the floor and folded the towel. "Maybe I should go to the news? I hate the idea of going public, but it would put some pressure on the chief and maybe someone from the surrounding counties will recognize her."

Going public was a bad idea. Janet had already reported the attack, and Todd feared if she kicked up a fuss, the assailant might decide letting her go had been a huge mistake.

"Do you have a copy of the sketch?" he asked.

She nodded. "I took a photo with my cell at the police station yesterday."

"Send it to me. An army buddy I served with opened her own private investigation firm. Charlie's incredible and has lots of connections in Texas. Maybe she can find out who the woman is."

Her whole face lit up right before she wrapped her arms around him. "That would be amazing."

The hug was meant to be friendly, but Todd's heart sputtered like his old truck's engine. Janet smelled like a field of wildflowers and the soft strands of her hair tickled his cheek. Alarm bells clanged in his head, and he gently extracted himself under the guise of sending his friend Charlie a text.

Yesterday's events had shaken him, as had the depth of his feelings. He never should have stayed in town so long, and now with Janet in danger, he couldn't leave until it was certain she was safe.

"You know, we can also go and chat with Mrs. Bertrand ourselves," he suggested, once he'd sent the message to Charlie. "Maybe she didn't see anything last night, but the chief may not have questioned her thoroughly. She might know something without realizing it."

"Good idea. I'll take some cinnamon rolls with me. She loves them."

His stomach rumbled. "Got one for me?"

"Of course."

He followed her into the renovated kitchen. He snagged a cinnamon roll for himself and guzzled another cup of coffee while she prepared a plate for the neighbor. A few minutes later, they were back outside, sans Callie, who watched with mournful brown eyes from the window as they went down the driveway.

"You did a great job on the kitchen, by the way," Janet said, as they crossed into the neighbor's property.

"With everything going on, I didn't have a chance to tell you."

"Thanks. The bathroom's next, so—"

The unmistakable sound of a shotgun being pumped cut him off. Todd whirled, guarding Janet with his body. An overweight man with a tangled beard stepped out from behind a tree and hefted the weapon to his meaty shoulder.

Todd raised his hands. "Hold on—"

"You're on my property."

"Buck?" Janet poked her head around from behind him. "What are you doing?"

Mrs. Bertrand's son. Todd had never met him, but Buck had been in and out of trouble with the law for years and suffered from mental health issues.

"I'm guarding my land. You're trespassing." He glared. "Who are you?"

"He's my friend and a new neighbor, Todd Duncan." Janet edged out from behind his back. "He's helped your mom out a couple of times by fixing things around the property."

"Todd, huh? You repaired the fence on the west end."

"I did."

The burly man grunted and then lowered his shotgun until the barrel was pointing at the ground. Todd's stomach muscles relaxed, but he kept on alert, unwilling to give Buck the benefit of the doubt.

"I'm sorry. We didn't mean to startle you." Janet lifted the plate in her hand. "We came to give your mother some pastries."

"She's sleeping. She hasn't been feeling well, but I can take them up to the house for you."

"I'm sorry to hear your mom's sick. I was hoping to talk to her. Do you think I could stop by later?"

"You wanna discuss the incident from last night, huh? The chief was already over here." He scratched his unruly beard with a dirty hand. "Did you get hurt?"

"No, but I'm worried about the woman who disappeared."

"Sorry, I can't help you out. Mom and I didn't see anything."

The Bertrand property was thick with trees, the road hidden from view almost as soon as someone wandered off the driveway. Since the attack happened at night, and during a thunderstorm, it wasn't unreasonable to believe it'd gone unnoticed.

"When did you get into town?" Todd asked.

"Last week."

From the way Janet's mouth tightened, the information was news to her. He also hadn't heard about Buck being back. Sweetgrass wasn't tiny, but neighbors kept an eye on each other. Had the man been hiding out? Could he be responsible for the attack on Janet? Possibly.

"Where were you last night?"

The other man's shoulders stiffened under his overalls. "Here. Taking care of my mother. We were tucked in the house, watching TV."

"Have you seen anything strange since coming back home?" His gaze dropped to the shotgun. "Any people wandering the property that shouldn't have been?"

"Just you two." He gestured to Janet for the plate and she obliged by handing it over. "I'll let my mom know you stopped by."

"If you see anything, Buck, please call the police." Janet bit her lip. "I'm worried about the missing woman."

He grunted but said nothing. Todd placed a hand on the small of Janet's back and led her back down the drive, keeping his body between hers and the shotgun.

He felt the weight of Buck's stare boring into him until they turned the corner.

FIVE

"Are you sure about this?" Todd asked, as they weaved their way through the pet expo in downtown Houston's convention center two days later. "The woman in the sketch might not be Valerie Coons. Charlie said the family never filed a missing persons report."

"I know." Janet scanned the faces around them, fear nipping at her heels as she moved farther into the crowd. "But it looks close enough to be her twin. I'd like to see what a member of the family thinks."

A large stage on their right was being set up for a presentation, and the air was scented with a mixture of cologne and the hot dogs being served at the cafeteria. Janet tucked an errant curl back under the silk scarf with trembling fingers. It was a sorry excuse for a disguise, but it was the best she could come up with at short notice.

A Huntington Pharmaceuticals sign hung above a corner booth. Easels with different animals ranging from dogs to cows were on display along with a list of products the company manufactured. Lacey Huntington, the CEO, was in the back of the booth eating a salad and studying her phone.

"Want me to come with you?" Todd asked.

"No." Janet let out a breath. "She's more likely to speak with me if I'm alone."

"I'll stick close. Whistle if you need me."

She nodded and straightened her shoulders. It was risky talking to Valerie's stepdaughter in such a public place, but Janet wasn't sure who to trust. Showing up at the corporate offices could've tipped off the attacker. Janet hoped the sheer number of people at the expo would help shield the interaction as merely business.

She darted around a couple of Huntington employees and beelined straight for Lacey. The other woman glanced up from her phone, the fork hovering halfway to her mouth, and frowned. She scanned Janet's blouse, probably looking for a name tag.

"Hi. I'm sorry." Lacey lifted the phone. "I'm in the middle of preparing for our company's presentation at the main stage, but I'm sure one of my other employees can help you."

"No, they can't." Janet reached into her purse and pulled out a printout of the sketch. "I need to talk to you about your stepmother, Valerie. Is this her?"

Lacey glanced down at the drawing and her perfectly arched brows lifted. "Where did you get this?"

Janet took a fortifying breath. *Please, Lord, help me*

find the words. Quickly, and in a low whisper, she told Lacey about the attack.

"Is this some kind of sick joke?" Lacey's cheeks grew pink and she half rose from the stool. "Because if it is—"

"It's not a joke. Please, you need to listen to me. You can call the Sweetgrass Police Department and verify my story. I filed a police report detailing the entire incident, although I didn't know the woman's name. Look at the drawing. It has the officer's name and the date."

Lacey scanned the drawing again and sank back down to the stool. "I don't understand."

Janet glanced around to ensure no one was paying attention to them. Todd stood within shouting distance, scanning the crowd. His beat-up leather jacket and steel-toed work boots were out of place in the sea of business attire. Seeing him there, standing guard, bolstered her courage.

She turned her attention back to the other woman and whispered, "I think your stepmother is in trouble."

"That's impossible." Lacey shoved her half-eaten salad to the side. "Valerie is traveling in Europe."

Janet's stomach churned. Did they have the wrong woman? It seemed hard to believe. Even Lacey thought the drawing was of Valerie.

"When did she leave?"

"Two weeks ago. My father..." She bit her lip and blinked rapidly. "My father died six months ago, and Valerie took it hard."

Marcus Huntington had passed away from a sudden heart attack. The announcement had been in one of the articles the private investigator had forwarded on. The company he'd built from the ground up went to his daughters, Lacey and her younger sister Katherine, in equal share.

"I'm sorry."

Lacey cleared her throat. "Thank you. Anyway, Valerie needed a change of scenery, and she's taking a three-month trip around Europe. I've been in contact with her since she left via email and text."

She pulled up an app on her phone and did a search. Correspondence between her and Valerie flashed across the screen. The last one was sent yesterday. They gave Janet pause, but email and text were easy to fake.

"What about by phone?"

"We don't normally speak. We're both busy, and with the time difference..." She fiddled with a sapphire ring on her finger. "Why am I even explaining this to you—?"

"Your stepmother—your family—is worth a lot of money." Janet kept her gaze locked on the other woman's face. "If someone has kidnapped her, and she momentarily escaped, it would explain how she ended up on the road that night. Have you received any demands for ransom?"

Something flickered in Lacey's expression. A slight twist of her mouth so fleeting, Janet would have missed it if she hadn't been looking for it.

Bingo.

"No one has contacted me." Lacey's chin tilted up. "My stepmother is fine and this conversation is over."

Janet placed a hand on the other woman's arm. The

muscles underneath the silk fabric were rigid. With fear? Or with something else?

Janet pitched her voice low. "You need to go to the police. If she's being held in Sweetgrass, then it gives us a starting point to find her."

Lacey shook off her hand. "I'll say it again, Valerie is fine and—"

"Sis?"

Both women jumped at the interruption. Katherine Huntington stood off to the side, her full lips pulled into a frown. The cerulean-colored pantsuit matched her eyes and, when she brushed a strand of blonde hair off her face, the diamond ring on her wedding finger shimmered.

"I'm sorry to interrupt, but Lee has arrived and we need to head over to the stage for our presentation." Her gaze flickered to Janet and her brow creased. "Have we met?"

Janet opened her mouth, but Lacey cut her off with a glare.

"No, Ms. West just had a few questions about our products. Unfortunately, we aren't able to help her." Her mouth tightened. "Now, if you'll excuse us."

She scooped up her phone and steered her sister away. Katherine passed a glance over her shoulder toward Janet as the two women crossed to a man standing near a large easel. Something about him looked familiar...

He turned to brush a kiss across Katherine's cheek. Janet gasped.

It was Lee Maxwell, Officer Winston Maxwell's brother.

Katherine said something, and Lee cast a glance over his shoulder. Janet was frozen, caught in the moment like a deer in the headlights, when he spotted her. His expression hardened and Lee's glare iced her blood.

He'd recognized her.

SIX

Todd's hands tightened on the steering wheel as the sign for Sweetgrass appeared. He debated continuing on the freeway. The urge to put distance between Janet and whatever she'd stumbled into was overwhelming.

After seeing Lee Maxwell with the Huntington sisters, they'd gone to the state police. The special agent was a friend of Janet's brother, and he'd promised to investigate further. It did little to ease Todd's nerves. They couldn't be sure who was involved or to what extent. Lee's brother worked for Sweetgrass Police Department and Todd wasn't willing to ignore the possibility the two siblings could be working together. Involving the state police, while the right thing to do, might've made Janet more of a target.

In the passenger seat next to him, Janet scowled and huffed an exaggerated sigh. She switched the cell phone to her other ear.

"I'm not flying to Nashville, Grady. Lauren already

has you there. One pesky sibling is enough." She paused. "No do *not* call Mom and Dad. They haven't been on vacation in ten years. It's their wedding anniversary. I've already called my friend Tara, and she's agreed to spend the night. Todd will also stay at the house, so we'll have protection."

There was a bit more negotiating before Janet sighed again and said, "Grady wants to talk to you. Do you mind if I put him on speaker?"

"No."

"Todd, I've heard good things about you from my folks, but Janet's my kid sister. If she gets hurt—"

"I won't let that happen, Grady. You have my word."

A deep-seated anger had been building inside him from the moment he'd discovered Janet drugged in her vehicle. Finding Valerie was only part of the equation. Todd wasn't going to stop until the man who'd put his hands on Janet was in a concrete cell with bars. It was his mission and one he gladly accepted.

He wouldn't let anyone hurt her.

Grady was silent for a beat. "Good. I expect if something happens, you will keep me updated."

"Of course," Janet answered, rolling her eyes. "Bye, Grady."

She hung up and tossed the phone in her bag. "Brothers."

"He cares about you. He's worried."

"I know." She rubbed her forehead, as if a headache was forming. "It didn't help matters when he found out Lee Maxwell could be involved. Since Katherine and Lee are engaged, there's a direct connection between Valerie and someone from Sweetgrass."

"Do you think Lee is capable of kidnapping a woman and holding her for ransom?"

"I don't know." She bit her lip. "The Maxwell brothers came from a wealthy family, but their father had a gambling problem and lost it all. After the bank repossessed their house, my father offered them both a job on our ranch." She knotted her hands together in her lap. "Things started disappearing afterward. Some cash here and there, my mother's watch."

"They were stealing from you."

"Yes. They also placed a couple of items in a ranch hand's room to frame him for it. I was the one who caught them and ratted them out."

He hit the steering wheel. "That little weasel Winston had the gall to accuse you of lying. I was mad about it then, but I'm furious now."

"Being a jerk isn't against the law. And, while stealing is serious, it's a far cry from kidnapping a woman and holding her for ransom."

As much as he didn't want to, Todd had to agree with her. Still...the kidnapping theory made sense, and Lee's connection to the family through Valerie's stepdaughter couldn't be a coincidence.

"Do you think Katherine and Lee are working together?"

She spread her hands. "It's possible. They're engaged. Of course, Lee could also be working on his own and Katherine has no idea."

"What about Lacey?"

"I think she knows her stepmother is in trouble. I wouldn't be surprised to learn she's the person the kidnapper has been demanding a ransom from."

Todd turned onto the street leading to Janet's house. "Why wouldn't she go to the police?"

"Maybe she's scared. The kidnapper may have threatened to kill Valerie if she involved the police. Honestly, I'm not sure we should have gone. I know the special agent promised to keep the investigation quiet, but I'm worried we made things worse."

"There's no way to know for sure. At least now there are more people looking for Valerie."

Janet nodded. "Can you drive past my house onto the back road? Valerie has been gone for a week, but I ran into her two days ago. If we are right, and she's been kidnapped for ransom, she must have escaped that night."

When Todd arrived at the location, she hopped out of the truck and studied both sides of the tree-lined street. "Valerie was running from somewhere and the attacker was chasing her. So where did they come from? And where did they go?"

"The chief mentioned the search dogs didn't pick up on anything, so they might not have left on foot. Is it possible there was a car but you didn't hear it?"

"I suppose. There was a thunderstorm and I was focused on helping Valerie. If it drove up with the headlights off..." She stared at the asphalt and frowned.

"What is it?" he asked.

"Valerie was trying to tell me something."

She took a few more steps, close to where Todd recalled her jacket being in the road on the night of the attack. Her shoulders stiffened. "What was it? Mail? Fail? No, none of that makes sense." She hit her thigh with a balled fist. "Why can't I remember?"

He closed the distance between them and clasped her shoulders. "Don't be so hard on yourself. You were drugged and terrified."

"Valerie's being held by a monster and I can't help her."

She turned, and Todd pulled her into his arms, brushing his hand over her riot of curls. They were silky against his palm. Her body trembled and it ripped at his heart.

"You aren't in this alone, Janet. We'll figure it out."

She lifted her face from his chest. Tears raced down her cheeks, smearing her makeup. Todd cupped her face and brushed them away with the pads of his thumbs. Her breath hitched, and the touch between them shifted from comforting to something different. Something electric. His heart kicked into high gear when her gaze dropped to his mouth.

Todd couldn't resist her any more than he could stop pulling air into his lungs. For the first time since he was sixteen, he ignored all common sense and his fears.

He kissed her.

SEVEN

Janet was in dangerous territory.

The warmth of Todd's lips, the gentleness of his touch, seared into her. The birds chirping in the trees, the rustle of the wind scattering the dried leaves, the horrible memory of the attack all melted away. In his arms emotions ruled, and there wasn't room for anything else.

She needed to tread lightly. Her feelings for Todd went far deeper than she'd allowed herself to admit. But he was leaving Sweetgrass, and if she wasn't careful, he was going to take her heart with him.

A branch broke in the woods behind Todd, and a flash of blue ducked behind a bush. She stiffened, any sense of momentary security fleeing.

"Buck," she whispered.

Todd peered into the woods before pushing her toward the vehicle. "Let's go."

He didn't have to tell her twice. Buck spying on them was beyond creepy. Todd's truck rumbled to life, and

Janet let out a sigh of relief when her house came into view.

"Is it possible Buck's involved in Valerie's disappearance?" Todd asked, as he shut off the engine. "He showed up in town right after Valerie went missing, he's guarding the property like he's got something to hide, and he's watching us. It's weird."

"I don't see how. Buck and the Maxwells don't get along at all. I can't see them working together."

"Maybe we're making the wrong assumption and the Maxwells aren't involved at all."

"But Buck doesn't have a connection to Valerie."

"How do you know?" he asked. "How much do you really know about him and where he's been in the last few years? Houston isn't far from Sweetgrass. It's conceivable Buck and Valerie could've crossed paths."

Goose bumps pebbled across her arms, and she hugged herself. "That's true."

"Valerie could be on the Bertrands' property."

Her throat clogged as the memory of the attacker covering her mouth swelled. The cab of the truck closed in. Her hand shook as she fumbled with the door handle before clambering out.

What was happening to Valerie right now? Had she been hurt when the SUV hit her? What about afterward?

Todd came around the vehicle. "I'm sorry. I have the sensitivity of a two-by-four."

"No, you didn't say anything I wasn't already thinking. It's just horrific. All of it. I feel so helpless."

"Would prayer help?"

She let out a breath, and tears burned the back of her eyes. "Yes, it would."

They joined hands, bowed their heads, and Janet poured all of the mixed emotions into her prayer. The weight crushing her shoulders lifted. Valerie was in God's hands. It didn't mean Janet would stop trying to find her or pushing law enforcement to help, but there was only so much she could control. The rest she had to give to the Lord.

After the prayer was done, she hugged Todd. "Thank you. I needed the reminder."

Arms wrapped around each other's waists, they walked to the house. Janet opened the door and silence greeted her.

"Callie?" Her heart skipped a beat, and she took several steps into the living room. The dog bed was empty. The curtains in the living room fluttered. Janet whirled and raced into the kitchen. Todd called out to her, but she didn't stop.

The back door was open.

She grabbed the counter for support as the room tilted. Mud smears marred the freshly laid tile, but with growing horror, she realized none of them were paw prints.

Janet bolted from the kitchen into the yard. "Callie!"

Todd caught up with her and grabbed onto her arm, halting her progress forward. He scanned the trees bordering her property. "Janet, it's not safe."

"I'm not leaving without my dog. She would never go far on her own."

She yelled again and again, Todd joining in, but Callie didn't appear. Tears blurred Janet's vision. If someone was willing to kidnap a woman, and attack another, what would he do to a dog?

"If she was somewhere outside, and heard me, she would come running." She swallowed past the sudden lump in her throat. "We have to organize a search for her. She could be hurt, or worse."

"Don't panic yet. Let's start in the storage sheds. If someone came into the house and let her outside, she may have gone exploring and gotten herself trapped. She's done it before."

It was logical, but Janet was beyond reason. Callie was a member of her family, and she had the horrible feeling something bad had happened to her beloved pet. She pitched forward, urgency fueling her strides.

Todd grabbed her hand. "Stay with me. I know you're scared for Callie, but it's safer if we're together."

"Okay, but please hurry."

They crossed the yard together. The rickety storage sheds sat along the tree line in a corner of the property. Todd's gaze scanned the area once more before he turned his attention to the first shed's windows. They were grimy with years of dust.

Janet wrapped her arms around her middle and stifled the urge to scream. Todd swung the door open.

Empty.

They moved to the next one. Janet's shoulder muscles ached and her teeth ground together, but a tingle on the back of her neck caused her to turn around. She scanned the tree line. Nothing. Behind her, the shed door creaked open and Todd inhaled sharply.

She whirled. Golden fur stood out against the cement floor and Janet pushed past Todd.

"Callie." Tears ran down her face as she dropped to her knees. Her poor dog had been hogtied. Duct tape was wrapped around her muzzle. Callie whimpered, and Janet hugged her.

"Todd, find me something to cut her free."

"I'll have a knife in my truck. We'll tend to her there." His voice was thick with emotion, and when he hefted the sixty-pound animal into his arms, fierce anger shimmered in his eyes. "Let's get out of here, Janet."

She rose from the floor, her gaze moving from Callie and Todd. She gasped and took a step back, banging into a collection of discarded brooms. They clattered into bits of broken lawn equipment before crashing to the floor.

Hanging from a wooden beam by a noose was a doll with an uncanny resemblance to Janet. Curly hair and a heart-shaped face dressed in jeans and cowboy boots. Duct tape sealed her mouth and in her hands was a sign.

SHUT UP.

The message was written in blood.

EIGHT

Chief Jackman's face was etched in granite when he exited the shed with Todd. Janet watched the men cross the yard from the window, Callie at her side. The Labrador mix had been thoroughly checked by the vet and, other than being a bit dehydrated, was unharmed. Unable to stomach returning home, they'd spent the night at her friend's house, but Janet's sleep had been restless.

Footsteps on the kitchen tile preceded their entry into the living room. She tensed, turning to greet the chief with a glare. "Now do you believe me?"

"I always believed you."

"Actually, your officer accused Janet of lying." Todd came to stand next to her, patting Callie on the head before placing his hand on the small of her back. His jaw clenched as he glared at the lawman. "And you insinuated she hallucinated the entire thing. From where I'm standing, it sure seems like you didn't believe her."

His words, along with the warmth of his touch, soothed the raw edges of her nerves. Janet didn't need him to fight her battles, but it was nice to have him as backup.

Jackman frowned. "There is still no evidence of the attack other than Janet's statement. I don't even have an ID on the missing woman."

"It's Valerie Coons."

"The state police went to speak to the Huntingtons last night. Both of them admit the woman in the sketch resembles their stepmother, but they swear can't be Valerie because she's traveling in Europe."

"Did the special agent talk to Valerie?" she asked.

"No. They promised to pass on the special agent's phone number and have Valerie call him as soon as possible."

"That's not good enough."

He threw up his hands. "What would you have me do? They're her family and they haven't reported her missing."

"Regardless, there is a woman out there being held by someone. Why won't you look for her? Are you afraid of what you will find if you do?"

He glowered. "I don't take kindly to you accusing a member of my department without evidence."

"Lee Maxwell is engaged to Valerie's stepdaughter, Winston is his brother, and I nearly ran over a woman who bears a striking resemblance to Valerie. What more do you need?"

"Actual physical evidence." His mouth pursed. "I will

have a forensic team come out to the house. I'll also send the sketch to law enforcement all over Texas. Maybe someone will recognize her."

Janet crossed her arms over her chest. "Don't be surprised if you get calls identifying her as Valerie Coons."

Todd's leg bounced up and down as he waited for his friend, Charlene "Charlie" Greer, to doctor her coffee. The private investigator used three spoons of sugar before drowning the dark brew in milk.

"How did you ever make it in the army?" he asked.

"I can rough it, soldier, if I have to." She smiled, flashing perfect white teeth before biting into an oatmeal raisin cookie. "Yum. This is amazing."

"Thank you." Janet placed a hand on his leg to stop the motion, and he took the opportunity to hold her hand. Their fingers interlocked. She edged closer to him until her shoulder brushed his. "So, how do you know Valerie has been kidnapped for sure?"

"Because Lacey Huntington has been sending money for the last two weeks to an offshore account. Not enough to draw attention, although the contact I spoke to said it was highly unusual activity for her."

Todd didn't know whether to feel sorry for the woman or be enraged she was hiding important information from the police. "Lacey's trying to handle this on her own."

"Looks like it, and although I can't be sure, I do have my doubts about Lee Maxwell's involvement."

"Why?"

"Because Katherine Huntington is a wealthy woman in her own right who doesn't believe in prenups. Once Lee marries her next month, he'll be set for life."

Janet sat back in her chair and sighed. "Well, there goes my number-one suspect."

Charlie licked cookie crumbs off her fingers, reached into her bag, and pulled out a file folder. "Well, let me replace it for you. Buck Bertrand and Valerie Coons are connected. After his last stint in prison—for aggravated assault, mind you—he worked for a landscaping company. One of their clients was Valerie."

She flipped to some documents. "According to work records, he went to her house every day for nine months, starting last year. He disappeared for a while afterward. I'm still tracking down where he was during that time. However, we do know he mysteriously arrives home after two years just as Valerie goes missing."

Todd pulled the folder closer and scanned the pages. Charlie's research was thorough. He flipped through Buck's criminal record. "He's been in and out of jail a lot."

"Most of his adult life. Not all of the charges stuck, but several of them are violent offenses. He's bad news and, in my opinion, capable of holding a woman for ransom." Charlie popped the last bit of cookie in her mouth and rose. "I'll keep digging, but I hope this helps."

"It helps a ton, Charlie." Janet hugged the other

woman. "I'll forward this on to the special agent we talked with at the state police. Maybe it'll encourage him to follow up with the Huntingtons."

Todd opened the front door. The porch light flickered on and illuminated the drive as he walked Charlie to her car.

"I like her. Don't screw it up."

"It might be too late." He rubbed the back of his neck. "I care about Janet. A lot. But her life is here, and I haven't lived in one place since I was sixteen years old."

Charlie sighed. "Todd, I'm going to tell you something I should have long ago but you weren't ready to hear. It's time to stop running."

"I'm not *running*. I like moving. Seeing new places and exploring the world."

"You're running," she answered flatly. "From your parents' car accident, from their deaths, from building a home and a life because you're scared to lose it all again."

He took a step back as if she'd slugged him. Each word burrowed deep into his heart and lodged there, ripping open scars he'd buried but not forgotten.

"Todd, the life you've been living is a Band-Aid, but it's not for the long haul. Your parents wouldn't want you to be alone forever. God doesn't either. Maybe He put Janet in your life because it's time for a change."

A thousand frames of his parents flickered through his mind in a matter of seconds. Their happiness so solid and real...until it wasn't. Gone, snuffed out by a drunk driver, within seconds.

He swallowed the lump in his throat. "I don't know if I can."

She pointed to the window. "You see that?"

He turned. Inside, Janet sat on the couch. Her curly hair was pulled back from her exquisite face and the cutest creases formed between her brows as she studied something on her phone. Next to her, Callie sat close, the dog's head resting on her owner's lap. All around them was the chaos of renovations. A ladder in the corner, his toolbox on the floor.

"That's your future," Charlie said. "Right in front of you. A woman who loves you. Someone you can build a life with."

His breath hitched.

"If you're not brave enough to grab onto it with both hands..." She shook her head. "Well, more the fool you."

NINE

"Are you sure about this?" Janet adjusted the goggles on her face and frowned. "I do want the wall gone, but I wasn't expecting to do it tonight."

"It's better than sitting around waiting for the phone to ring." Todd picked up the sledgehammer and handed it to her. "We've forwarded the information to the state police and the chief. There's nothing more we can do for Valerie right now, which leaves us twiddling our thumbs."

The man had a point. She tested the weight of the sledgehammer. Todd took several steps back, and she slammed into the drywall. It caved. She did it again and again, until she was panting and sweat dripped down her back.

"Feel good?" He grinned at her, his dimple winking.

"Yes." She smiled back, grabbed a piece of drywall, and ripped it off. "You were right. I needed to take my mind off everything."

"And the best part is, after we're done, we get to make something better."

Janet yanked another piece of drywall down. She peered into the space. "Hey, Todd, there's a room inside the wall and...is that a door in the floor?"

She ran to get a flashlight while Todd tore down enough of the wall so they could get inside the hidden room. It wasn't big, maybe six feet by six feet, just enough to hide the metal door in the floor. Something tugged at the back of Janet's memory, but she couldn't quite catch it.

"How weird." Todd bent down and grasped the handle. The hinges creaked and groaned, revealing a set of metal stairs. "A root cellar? Or a basement?"

"They aren't common in Texas." She gasped. "Jail! Todd, that's what Valerie was trying to tell me."

"You lost me."

"This property used to be the site of the old Sweetgrass courthouse, and the jail was on

the opposite side of the road. They built a passageway under Main Street to transport the prisoners from one to the other for safety reasons. When a hurricane took out the entire town, it moved locations to the present-day one." She shone the flashlight into the gaping hole in the floor. "This must be the old passageway, and there should be a door on the other side hidden somewhere on the Bertrands' property."

He inhaled sharply. "It's where Valerie is being held."

Janet tossed aside her goggles and started down the stairs. Todd grabbed her arm.

"Hold on. We aren't going anywhere until we tell the police."

"Who? The chief is the closest, and he hasn't been much help so far. Besides, we don't know for sure she's down there. We just *think* she is."

The chief wasn't going to rush over on a hunch, and Janet wasn't going to leave Valerie down there for one minute more than necessary.

"Wait." Todd disappeared from view and came back with a large knife. "Let me lead the way."

She shone the light on the stairs, guiding his path, before following him down. The corridor was wide enough for three men, and Janet had no trouble imagining two jailers, with a prisoner walking between them, traveling the route. Their footsteps whispered against the concrete and spiderwebs clung to the corners. She shivered as the dampness embraced her.

Todd adjusted his hold on the knife. "Make sure you stay behind me."

Together, they crept down the corridor. Sweetgrass Jail was stamped into the concrete at regular intervals. Dust particles danced in the beam of the flashlight. Janet's nose burned and she scrunched it, stifling the urge to sneeze.

Todd drew up short. He placed a finger to his lips before reaching out to click off the flashlight. Darkness enveloped them. Her heart thundered against her ribs, and she held her breath, straining to hear.

Faint voices filtered down the corridor.

Some decisions were instinctive.

Continuing forward held risks, but so did returning back to Janet's house. There was no guarantee they wouldn't be discovered either way. There was also Valerie to consider. Todd had promised to protect Janet, but he also wouldn't leave a vulnerable woman on her own with a monster. If there was any way to help Valerie, he needed to try.

Todd pressed Janet up against the wall and edged his way down the corridor toward the shaft of light. Each silent step brought the voices closer.

"I'm telling you, things are getting too hot. We need to take the money we've gotten from Lacey and let Valerie go."

"No! You promised me, Lee."

Janet tugged on the back of his shirt. She'd also identified both men by the name and the cadence of their speech.

Winston and Lee Maxwell.

"What we've gotten so far isn't enough. We were supposed to replace the fortune that would have been mine if Dad hadn't gambled it all away."

"And I will," Lee argued. "You'll have to be patient. At some point, after I'm married, Katherine will loosen the purse strings. Then I can slip you money."

"You mean you'll give me crumbs while you sit high

on the hog. No thank you. We made a deal, and I expect you to stick to it."

Todd's fingers ached from holding the knife handle, and he flexed his fingers. Was either man armed? Chances were, as an officer, Winston was. The blade would do them no good in a gunfight.

"What will you get if you're in prison, Winston? That West woman is poking around. Things are liable to spin out of control if we aren't careful. I've convinced Lacey to keep doing as she's been instructed by the kidnapper, but I'm afraid she's going to crack and tell the police everything."

"I already sent Janet a warning she won't forget. If it doesn't scare her into silence, then we'll get rid of her."

Todd's body temperature skyrocketed, and he ground his teeth together. Winston Maxwell was done.

Done.

He would make sure of it.

"What do you mean you sent her a warning?"

The panic in Lee's voice was palpable, but Todd felt no sympathy for the other man. He'd made a deal with the devil and now he was paying the price.

"Never you mind," Winston said. "Let's keep the lovely Mrs. Coons for two more weeks and we'll up the ransom amount. It should tide me over until you can start slipping me money from Katherine's pile."

Lee was silent for a long beat. "Fine. But, remember, no one gets hurt."

Winston made a noncommittal sound. "If you had

just killed Janet to begin with, we wouldn't be in this mess now."

Behind him, Janet inhaled sharply. So it had been Lee who attacked her the night Valerie escaped. He sent up a silent thanksgiving to God. If the circumstances had been different and Winston had been chasing Valerie, things would have gone a very different way.

"Let's get out of here. I'm starving." Winston's footsteps echoed down the corridor, moving away from them. "Is she locked up tight?"

"Of course."

"We'll send the email demanding more money tomorrow—"

A sneeze interrupted him. With horror, Todd realized it had come from Janet. She buried her face in his back and sneezed again.

Silence.

"Did you hear something?" Winston asked.

TEN

Janet's hand was slick against the plastic handle of the flashlight. The instinctual urge to flee battled with her rational common sense to stay as still as possible. Todd urged her closer behind him, until she was wedged between the concrete wall and the hard muscles of his back.

"I could have sworn I heard..."

"Come on, Winston. We've got to hurry before Buck comes back. He's been checking the property ever since the escape." Lee huffed. "Hasn't been home in two years and he shows up now. It's like we're cursed."

"Get a grip. He's an ex-con. All we have to do is threaten him."

Their footsteps faded, followed by the slam of a door. Janet released the breath she was holding.

Todd turned his head and whispered, "Let's wait a few minutes and make sure they are really gone."

Time stretched into an eternity. Her muscles tightened until she was afraid they would snap and crumble into powder. Finally, Todd inched along the wall bringing them closer to the light. The path dead-ended into a holding cell with a broken and rusted door.

The corridor continued on her right, but to the left was a door with a small window in the upper half. Janet grabbed the handle and tugged. To her surprise, it flew open, revealing a small room.

Valerie Coons was chained to the floor.

Valerie's eyes widened as her gaze darted back and forth between Janet and Todd. Her hair was dirty and tangled, her clothes muddy. The room reeked of sweat, waste, and stale french fries. For a long heartbeat, no one moved.

"I prayed and prayed..." Tears streamed down Valerie's face. "You found me."

"Yes, we did." Janet rushed to her side. "And now we're going to get you out of here."

She lifted her hands, bound by heavy chains. "I can't get these off."

"We need a bolt cutter," Todd said. "I have one at the house."

Valerie clung to Janet, clutching the fabric of her clothes in her hands. "Please don't leave me."

Even if she could wrestle herself free, could she bear to leave the other woman in the room, alone, for one extra minute? No. There wasn't a choice.

"Todd, go back to the house and get the cutter. Hurry. I'll stay here with Valerie."

He hesitated but seemed to recognize arguing would

be futile. He grabbed the flashlight from her outstretched hand and kissed her on the mouth. "I'll be right back."

Todd disappeared. Janet rearranged herself into a more comfortable position next to Valerie, keeping her arms around her. It was freezing cold in the room.

"He'll come back, right?"

"Absolutely. Are you injured?" She rubbed Valerie's arms up and down, trying to warm her. "Did I hurt you when I hit you with the car?"

"You didn't hit me. I thumped against the side of the vehicle when I fell. The drugs they gave me made it hard to run and my body couldn't go anymore." She licked her lips. "Other than a few bumps and bruises, I'm okay."

A knot uncoiled in Janet's chest and she breathed deep. Valerie was alive. They were going to get her out of here. Footsteps echoed against the concrete, and Janet squeezed Valerie.

"See, I told you he'd come back."

A man appeared in the doorway wearing a black ski mask and holding a gun. "You're right, I did."

Winston.

Valerie screamed. Janet clenched her teeth together to keep them from chattering but there was nothing she could do to stop the trembles running through her body. Winston yanked her out of the room and into the main area, tossing her up against the broken holding cell. Pain shot up her elbow.

"I knew I heard someone." Winston slammed the door, separating them from Valerie.

Footsteps on metal stairs preceded Lee entering the

space. He saw Janet and his mouth dropped open. "What...what is she doing here?"

The corridor connecting the area to Janet's house was dark. Todd hadn't had enough time to find the bolt cutters and come back. What was she going to do? She was no match for two men nor could she outrun a gun. Valerie's sobs seeped through the closed door.

"Does it matter how she got here?" Winston yanked off the ski mask covering his face. "We have to kill her."

The blood drained from Lee's face. "We said no one would get hurt."

Janet's heart leaped. Maybe there was a way...

"That was before. This is now." Winston held out the gun to his brother. "It'll be better if you do it."

Lee reared back. "Me? I'm not going to."

"Oh, yes you are. You should've killed her the first night. You created this mess and now you're going to clean it up."

"Don't do it." Janet swallowed hard. "Lee, he's tricking you. He's going to have you kill me so he can hold it over you. He'll blackmail you for the rest of your life."

Lee's gaze darted toward her before landing back on his brother.

Winston laughed. "Don't be absurd. We're in this together. Don't let her screw with your head."

"I'm not—"

"Shut up!"

Winston's hand shot out and slammed into Janet's stomach. She doubled over, tears blurring her vision. She couldn't breathe.

"Enough of this. Take the gun, Lee. Shoot her, and then I'll help you get rid of the body."

She lifted her head, wheezing. Beyond the strands of her hair, the gun barrel was a dark cavernous hole pointed straight at her. Winston backed up a step.

"Do it, Lee. Shoot her."

Janet shook her head. She forced her gaze up to Lee's face. Indecision warred and then he gritted his teeth.

Her death flashed in his eyes.

A blur of flannel and boots flew from the darkness of the corridor and tackled Lee. The gun clattered against the concrete and skittered across the smooth surface. Janet lunged and wrapped her fingers around the metal just as Winston slammed into her. The force of his momentum shoved her into the bars of the holding cell. Pain exploded across her shoulder and hip.

His meaty hand clamped down on her wrist, grinding the bones together. Janet cried out. Winston's mouth twisted into a sneer, spittle gathering at the corners. The blood rushing in her ears drowned out everything and instinct took over as she grappled for control of the gun wedged between them.

She couldn't let him have it. He would kill her.

"Sweetwater Police! Freeze! Everyone freeze!"

Winston smiled. He yanked on her fingers.

The gun fired.

ELEVEN

Three days later

"Winston's going to pull through." Chief Jackman shifted in his boots on Janet's front porch and fiddled with the sunglasses in his hand. "Of course, once he's finished recovering from the bullet wound, he'll be spending the next fifty years in prison with his brother, but I thought ya'll would want to know."

Todd squeezed her shoulders, and Janet let out the breath she was holding. She hated Winston's actions, and Lee's, but she wished neither man dead.

"I also came to apologize." He licked his lips. "I placed my trust in Winston and I shouldn't have. It blinded me to things and delayed the investigation. There's no excuse for it, and I hope you'll forgive me."

Janet had learned new things about the investigation in the intervening days. Winston hadn't just manipulated his brother, he'd done the same to his boss. When Janet made her original complaint, it was Winston who did the initial "investigation" and convinced the chief there was no physical evidence to back up her story. After the doll was left in her shed and the connection between Lee Maxwell and Katherine Huntington was revealed, Chief Jackman started to question his own officer. He followed Winston, attempting to see if he would lead him to the missing woman, but it had taken time to discover the door hidden on the Bertrands' property.

The chief arrived right before Winston attempted to wrestle the gun away, causing it to go off. Jackman had provided first aid until the ambulance arrived, saving Winston's life. Janet was grateful. Although she hadn't purposefully fired the gun, it would have haunted her to know Winston had died and she'd been a part of it.

"We've all been blinded by someone we care about." Callie nudged Janet's hand, and she ran her fingers through the dog's silky fur. "In the end you did the right thing. That's what matters."

Todd nodded. "There were a lot of mistakes made. If Lacey and her sister had told the truth about Valerie's disappearance, it would have made a difference as well."

"It's no excuse. I have to take the blame for my own actions or—in this case—inaction. I've apologized to Valerie as well and..." His voice choked off and he lowered his head. "She's given me grace I don't deserve."

Janet wasn't surprised. In the last few days, she'd spent a lot of time with Valerie and found her to be warm and generous. She wasn't going to recover overnight from the kidnapping, but with therapy and prayer, she'd get there.

With a wave, the chief got in his vehicle and drove away.

"Time to tackle your bathroom." Todd marched toward the front door. He paused and cast a glance over his shoulder. "Unless you have another crime up your sleeve you want help solving."

Janet laughed. "No, I'll leave the crime solving to the professionals from now on."

"Smart woman." He clapped his hands together and rubbed them in anticipation. "So, bathroom it is."

"About that..." She drew in a fortifying breath and tightened her hold on the railing. *Like the sledgehammer, swing and break it.*

"Listen, I know you stuck around to help me finish my renovation, but after everything, I wouldn't blame you for wanting to leave town. Nearly getting killed by crazy kidnappers wasn't part of our bargain. So, don't worry. You can go and there's no hard feelings. I'll hire someone else to finish the house..."

Janet realized she was rambling and forced herself to stop talking. Todd's boots thumped over the porch. She lifted her gaze from the floor, over his jeans and flannel shirt. Her hand, seemingly of its own accord, reached out to tug on the hem, straightening a wrinkle. She bit her lip as tears pricked her eyes.

"Actually, I was thinking of sticking around Sweetgrass."

She blinked. "You were?"

"Yeah."

His hand closed over hers, the calluses from years of hard work rubbing along the skin of her knuckles. He pressed her palm over the steady beat of his heart.

She swallowed hard, not quite daring herself to hope. "For how long?"

"Well, it depends." He ducked his head until she was forced to meet his gaze. "I've spent a long time running from love, but God had a plan to help me heal the whole time. I'm pretty sure it involves you and a future together."

She inhaled sharply, scanning his face. The curve of his lips, the stubble along his jaw, the flecks of gold in his dark eyes. She savored the moment, knowing it would be with her forever, a story to tell her grandchildren.

Todd bent his head and brushed his lips with hers. "So, the way I see it, the question isn't how long I'll stay. It's how long will you have me."

Her heart soared. "How does forever sound?"

"Sounds perfect to me."

AFTERWORD

From the moment Janet appeared in *Ranger Protection*, I knew she needed her own story. A few days later, I stumbled across the cover of this book, and the idea for the opening scene popped into my head. The rest, as they say, is history.

The tunnel underneath Janet's house was inspired by a true piece of Texas history. The Belknap Tunnel in Fort Worth was used to transport prisoners from the courthouse to the prison and vice versa in safety. The courthouse has since moved, and the tunnel has been sealed, but it's an interesting tidbit that was fun to include in my novel.

Thanks for reading!

ABOUT THE AUTHOR

Lynn Shannon worked as a family law attorney before becoming a full-time author. Her novels combine intriguing mysteries with heartfelt romance. You can learn more on her website www.lynnshannon.com

You can also follow her on social media at any of these sites.

Facebook: LynnShannonBooks
Twitter: @LynnSWrites
Instagram: lynnshannonauthor

Reviews help readers find books. Please consider leaving a review at your favorite place of purchase or anywhere you discover new books. Thank you.

Made in the USA
Monee, IL
23 June 2021